AUTUMN
PUBLISHING

Published in 2019
by Autumn Publishing
Cottage Farm
Sywell
NN6 0BJ
www.igloobooks.com

Autumn is an imprint of Bonnier Books UK

0919 001
2 4 6 8 10 9 7 5 3 1
ISBN 978-1-78905-554-2

Printed and manufactured in China

This book belongs to

Long ago, near the Enchanted Forest full of elemental spirits, a battle broke out between the Arendellians and the Northuldra, who were rumoured to be magical. The two sides fought against each other, however Prince Agnarr escaped and returned to Arendelle where he became king. But the fighting had angered the spirits, and for those still in the forest, an impenetrable mist rose up, trapping them forever.

As King Agnarr finished telling the story, Anna and Elsa hung on his every word. The young princesses loved listening to their parents' tales about the past. "Were the Northuldra really magical? Like me?" Elsa asked. Her father told Elsa that there was no one like her.

Their mother, Queen Iduna, sang a lullaby about a special river called Ahtohallan, said to hold all the answers about the past.

"Do you think Ahtohallan knows why I have powers?" asked Elsa.

"If Ahtohallan is out there, I imagine it knows that and much more," answered the queen.

"Someone should really try to find it," Elsa said, closing her eyes.

Later that night, Anna woke up and ran to the window. She looked outside at the Northern Lights before calling to Elsa: "The sky's awake, so I'm awake, so we have to play!"

Many years had passed since then, and though their parents were gone, lost in a shipwreck, Anna and Elsa grew incredibly close. One thing the sisters and their friends Kristoff, Olaf and Sven always made time for was family game night, and tonight they were playing charades. However, Anna struggled to guess what Elsa was acting out, and she knew something was bothering her sister. "Are you okay?" she asked.

"Just tired," said Elsa, forcing a smile. "Goodnight," she added, as she left and went to her room.

The truth was, something was bothering Elsa. A mysterious voice had been calling to her, trying to draw her away from the kingdom. It seemed as though no one else could hear it, and though she tried, she couldn't silence it.

Moments later, Anna appeared at the door. "You're wearing Mother's scarf," she said. "You do that when something's wrong."

Elsa didn't want to worry Anna, so she said, "I just don't want to mess things up."

Later that night, Elsa woke up to the sound of the voice calling to her once again. As much as she wanted to ignore it, Elsa couldn't help but feel curious. What did it want?

Elsa followed the voice to the fjord, and as she sang in response to it, a thought came to her. Tentatively she used her magic, tossing snow into the air. Images she had never seen before blossomed from her fingertips and surrounded her, forming the image of the Enchanted Forest her father spoke about when she was a child.

Fascinated by the imagery she had created, Elsa blasted out her magic, and an enormous shock wave swept across the fjord with a boom! The moisture in the sky froze into small crystals that hung suspended in the air. Elsa looked around, in awe of what she had done.

The deafening sound startled Anna awake, and she raced to the balcony looking for Elsa. As the sisters' eyes met, a blinding blast of light came from the north and the crystals dropped to the ground in a cascade.

Anna rushed through the village towards Elsa. As the crystals fell, Arendelle transformed. Water fountains dried up, the lanterns went out and the ground rippled like the sea to push the villagers out of their homes.

Once everyone was safe on the cliffs above Arendelle, Elsa told Anna about the voice. "What does it say?" Anna asked.

Elsa explained that the voice hadn't said anything, it had showed her the Enchanted Forest. Elsa knew she needed to travel there.

The ground began to rumble again, but this time it was the mountain trolls. Grand Pabbie went straight to Elsa. Both of them could feel that the spirits of nature were angry. "Much about the past is not what it seems," Pabbie said. "When one can see no future, all one can do is the next right thing."

Elsa knew she needed to find the voice. Her magic made her sure about going to the Enchanted Forest. But Elsa wouldn't be going alone. Her friends would join her.

Grand Pabbie motioned to Anna and told her that he would take care of the villagers, but she needed to watch over Elsa. "I won't let anything happen to her," Anna promised.

At dawn, Anna, Kristoff, Olaf and Sven joined Elsa, and they began their journey. They passed many places they had seen before and continued even further into the unknown. As the day turned to evening, everyone was tired of Olaf's ceaseless chatter.

Since learning to read, he had been full of facts and felt their trip was the perfect excuse to share them all. "Do you know that water has memory?" Olaf asked.

As the night came to an end, Elsa suddenly asked Kristoff to stop the sleigh. "I hear the voice," she said.

Up ahead, over a small rise in the road, was a vast wall of glittering mist. Elsa ran straight to it, knowing they had arrived. She stopped a safe distance away, saying nothing as her friends joined her. Kristoff tried to touch the mist, but his hand sprang back – it was bouncy.

Elsa reached for Anna's hand, drawing on her sister's strength. Slowly, the mist parted before them.

The mist continued to roll back, revealing four stone monoliths.
As they passed the pillars, the mist closed behind them, trapping the
group inside. The sparkling colours in the mist shifted and aligned,
then something about the mist changed. It was now pushing them.

They were propelled free of the mist and into a clearing. Olaf tried to touch the mist again but it had returned to being bouncy. "Okay, it let us in, but it clearly doesn't want to let us out," said Kristoff.

They found themselves in a beautiful forest. The towering trees had shimmering leaves and stretched towards the sky. The group slowed their pace, staggered by the beauty.

Suddenly, a huge gust of wind swept up Elsa and her friends. It was the Wind Spirit. Desperately, Elsa threw a steady stream of snow towards the centre of the vortex.

The wind swirled tighter around Elsa until, finally, she
opened her arms, blasting out her powers. Snow filled the air
and froze into beautiful ice sculptures. Each one appeared to
represent a moment in time. "Water has memory," Olaf said,
explaining how ice could reveal the past.

One of the sculptures immediately captured the sisters'
attention: young Prince Agnarr cradled in the arms of a girl!

Suddenly, they heard noises coming from the bushes. Anna broke off an ice sword from one of Elsa's sculptures. Before they knew it, they were surrounded by a group of people, including soldiers. It was the trapped Northuldra and Arendellians from King Agnarr's story!

Still at odds after so many years, the leader of the Northuldra, Yelana, bickered with the Arendellian lieutenant, Mattias. Anna took a step towards them, but they believed Anna was attacking.

Both the Northuldra and the Arendellians rushed
towards the group. Elsa used her powers to send them slipping
to the ground. "That was magic. Did you see that?" Mattias said.

"Of course I saw it," Yelana responded.

Ryder, a young Northuldra, introduced himself and his sister, Honeymaren, to Elsa and her friends.

Anna found herself staring at Mattias, trying to figure out where she knew him from. Finally, she blurted out, "Library, second portrait on the left. You were our father's official guard." Mattias was overjoyed to hear that their father was King Agnarr and that he had made it back to Arendelle all those years ago.

Yelana warned her people not to trust Elsa and accused her of sorcery. Anna explained that Elsa was not a sorcerer, but had been born with magic.

"But did you know that your grandfather, your king, despised magic?" Yelana asked.

"He only feared how people like you could exploit it!" Mattias responded. "The spirits themselves turned against you!"

"They turned against you, too! You are trapped here, too!" Yelana shouted back.

Suddenly, a bright flash of fire appeared.

"Fire Spirit!" Yelana yelled. A ball of fire dashed around a tree, sending it up in flames. Chaos erupted as it blazed a trail through the forest, burning everything in its path. Elsa raced behind it, using her magic to try to stop it from spreading. When she finally caught up with it, she saw that the Fire Spirit was actually a small salamander.

Looking deep into the Fire Spirit's eyes, Elsa understood its feelings of pain and fear. She gently held out her hand and it scampered onto her palm, enjoying her cool touch. As she helped it find calm, the flames died down.

Upset by what had happened, Elsa pulled out her mother's scarf and wrapped it round Anna, knowing it would comfort her. Ryder and Honeymaren were intrigued by it. Elsa explained that it had been a gift from their father to their mother.

Recognising the symbols on the scarf, Elsa looked at the ice sculpture she had made and realised the young girl was wearing the same one. The girl who saved their father had been Northuldra!

Later, over by the campfire, Honeymaren pointed out to Elsa the spirits of nature symbolized on the scarf. Elsa was surprised to discover there was a fifth spirit. It was said to connect the magic of nature to humans, and it disappeared when people stopped listening. Some of the Northuldra claimed they heard it crying out the day the forest fell.

Shortly after, Elsa realised she needed to go north right away, so she set off with Anna and Olaf close behind her.

Elsa led Anna and Olaf as she followed the mysterious voice. Soon they were looking down at an old Arendellian shipwreck, its tattered flag waving sadly. Anna and Elsa gasped at the sight, realising it was their parents' ship! They ran down to take a closer look. What was their ship doing there?

After searching the
ship, they found a map
that proved their parents
had been trying to reach
Ahtohallan, the special river
their mother told them about
as little girls in her lullaby.
Could it actually exist?
Suddenly, Elsa felt guilty that
they had died in an attempt
to learn why Elsa was born
with magic.

Elsa ran from the ship.
"This is my fault," she said,
near tears. Anna insisted
she wasn't responsible
and reminded Elsa of her
important quest. "If anyone
can save Arendelle, and free
this forest, it's you," she said.
"I believe in you, Elsa, more
than anyone or anything."

Elsa vowed to find Ahtohallan, but she had to do it alone. Anna
wanted to go with her, but Elsa magically created a boat under
Anna and Olaf and sent them zipping down a path of ice. Anna
scrambled, trying to stop their progress. She thought she had been
successful as the boat changed course and slid across dry land.
But when it dropped down a slope, Anna and Olaf slipped into a
river of sleeping Earth Giants and floated safely away.

Later, Elsa finally reached the north and stood at the edge of the Dark Sea. She tied up her hair, took a deep breath and sprinted towards the treacherous waves. She created large snowflakes underfoot to support her weight as she ran across the top of the rolling water. The waves quickly knocked her down. Elsa pulled herself back to the shore and attempted once more to cross the sea.

As another wave came towards her, she froze it and used it as a slide, but the next wave broke the slide and she dived into the water. She had no time to notice the enormous Water Nokk watching her.

Deep beneath the dark waters, the Water Nokk swam up to Elsa and looked her in the eye before disappearing. Elsa pulled herself to the water's surface and climbed onto an ice float she had created. The Water Nokk rammed the ice, breaking it and tossing Elsa back into the water.

The two battled, both above and under the sea. Elsa used her magic to make an ice bridle. She grabbed the reins and swung onto the Water Nokk's back. At first it bucked, but soon she was riding it to the opposite shore.

Once safely across the Dark Sea, Elsa removed the bridle from the Water Nokk. She had reached the end of her journey north. The voice had led her to her destiny, and finally fell silent. Elsa felt at ease. The journey had changed her, freed her. She had no doubt that the Enchanted Forest and all the people trapped inside would soon be free, too. Peace and harmony were finally going to be restored to the unbalanced land.

Across the sea, Anna and Olaf's boat landed them in lost caverns. They got out and explored their surroundings, illuminated by Anna's torch. Suddenly, an ice sculpture began to form before their eyes! They were relieved. This meant Elsa had made it across the Dark Sea!

Anna looked closely at the ice sculpture and she immediately knew why Elsa had sent it as a message. It explained what had happened when the Arendellians and Northuldra battled in the forest long ago. She wondered how she could correct all the wrongs of the past. Then, Anna remembered the advice given to her by Grand Pabbie – do the next right thing. And with that, Anna took a step forward to help save the kingdom...